MAZESCAPES

ROXIE MUNRO

SeaStar Books
NEW YORK

COME ALONG ON A TRIP TO THE ZOO—
there's so much to see and so much to do!

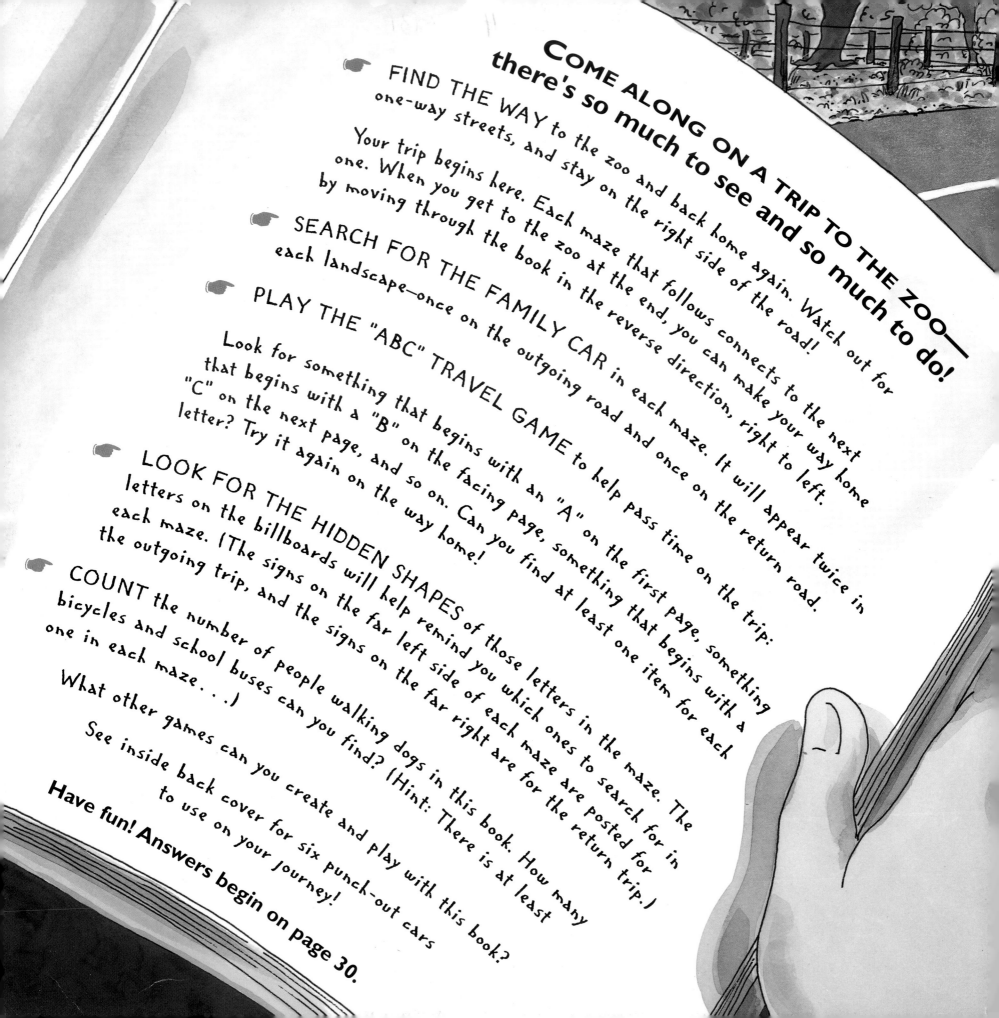

☞ **FIND THE WAY** to the zoo and back home again. Watch out for one-way streets, and stay on the right side of the road!

Your trip begins here. Each maze that follows connects to the next one. When you get to the zoo at the end, you can make your way home by moving through the book in the reverse direction, right to left.

☞ **SEARCH FOR THE FAMILY CAR** in each maze. It will appear twice in each landscape—once on the outgoing road and once on the return road.

☞ **PLAY THE "ABC" TRAVEL GAME** to help pass time on the trip: Look for something that begins with an "A" on the first page, something that begins with a "B" on the facing page, something that begins with a "C" on the next page, and so on. Can you find at least one item for each letter? Try it again on the way home!

☞ **LOOK FOR THE HIDDEN SHAPES** of those letters in the maze. The letters on the billboards will help remind you which ones to search for in each maze. (The signs on the far left side of each maze are posted for in the outgoing trip, and the signs on the far right are for the return trip.)

☞ **COUNT** the number of people walking dogs in this book. How many bicycles and school buses can you find? (Hint: There is at least one in each maze. . .)

What other games can you create and play with this book?

See inside back cover for six punch-out cars to use on your journey!

Have fun! Answers begin on page 30.

A N S W E R K E Y

SUBDIVISION
AB: ambulance, balloons
YZ: yard sale, zigzag road sign

Bicycles: 7
School Buses: 2
Dog Walkers: 7

TOWN
CD: clock, dock
WX: water tower, "X" (children crossing)

Bicycles: 7
School Buses: 7
Dog Walkers: 3

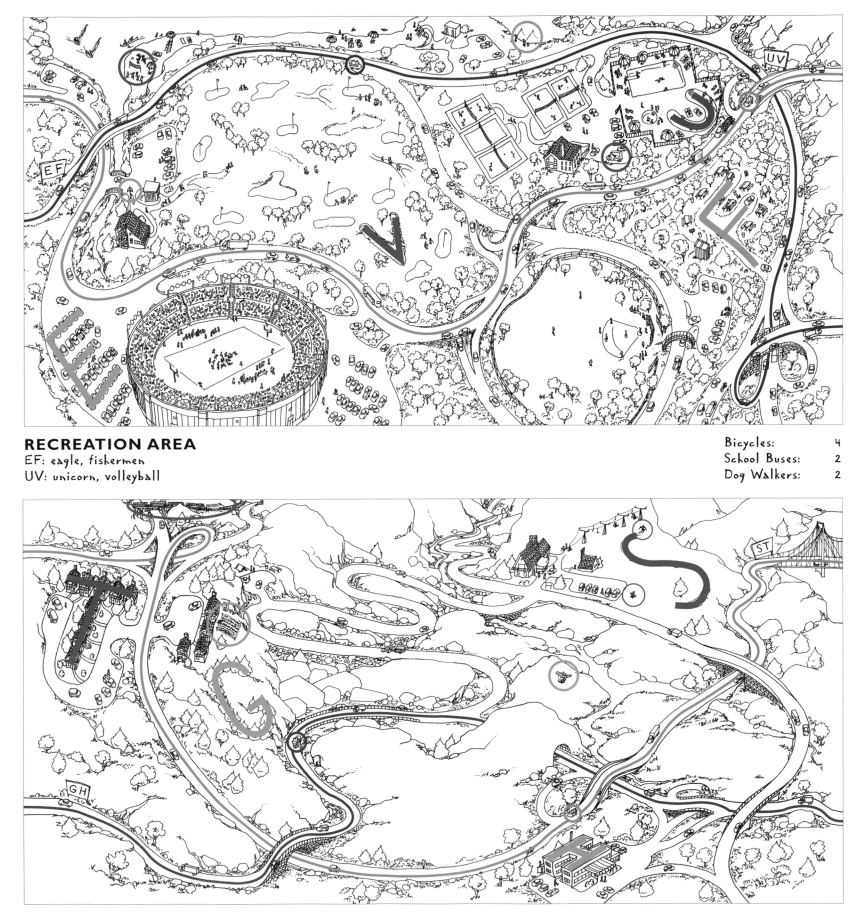

RECREATION AREA
EF: eagle, fishermen
UV: unicorn, volleyball

Bicycles: 4
School Buses: 2
Dog Walkers: 2

MOUNTAINS
GH: garden, hang glider
ST: skiers, train

Bicycles: 3
School Buses: 1
Dog Walkers: 1

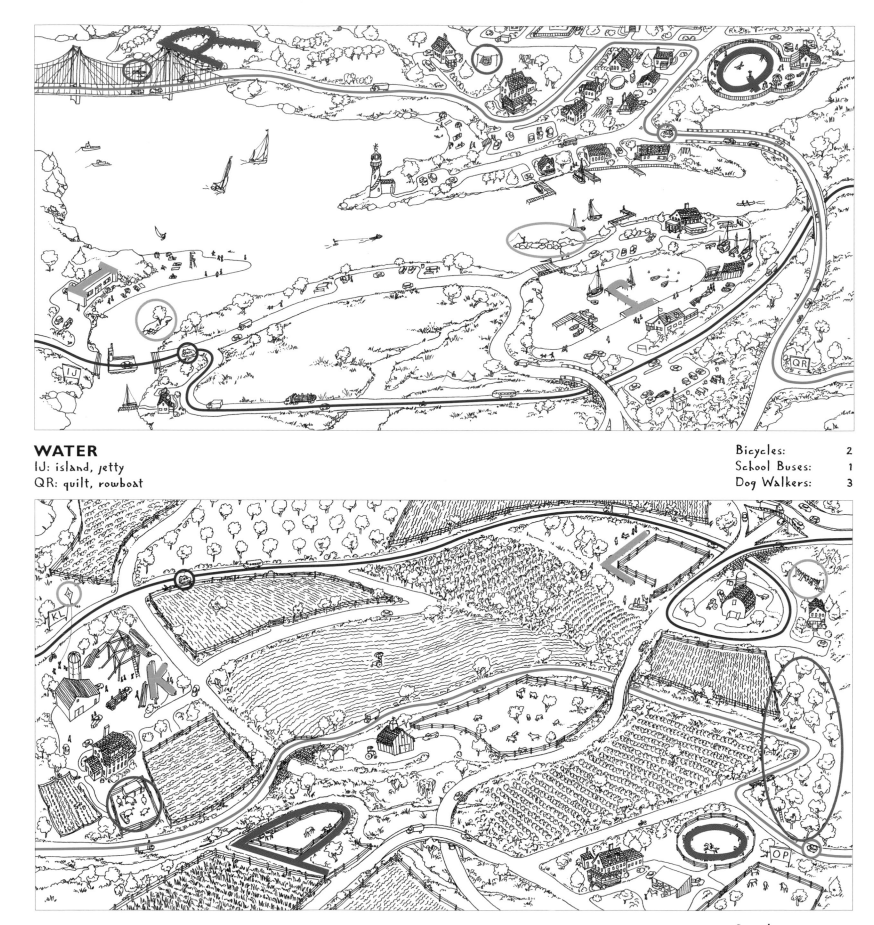

WATER
IJ: island, jetty
QR: quilt, rowboat

Bicycles:	2
School Buses:	1
Dog Walkers:	3

FARMS
KL: kite, laundry
OP: orchard, pigs

Bicycles:	2
School Buses:	1
Dog Walkers:	1

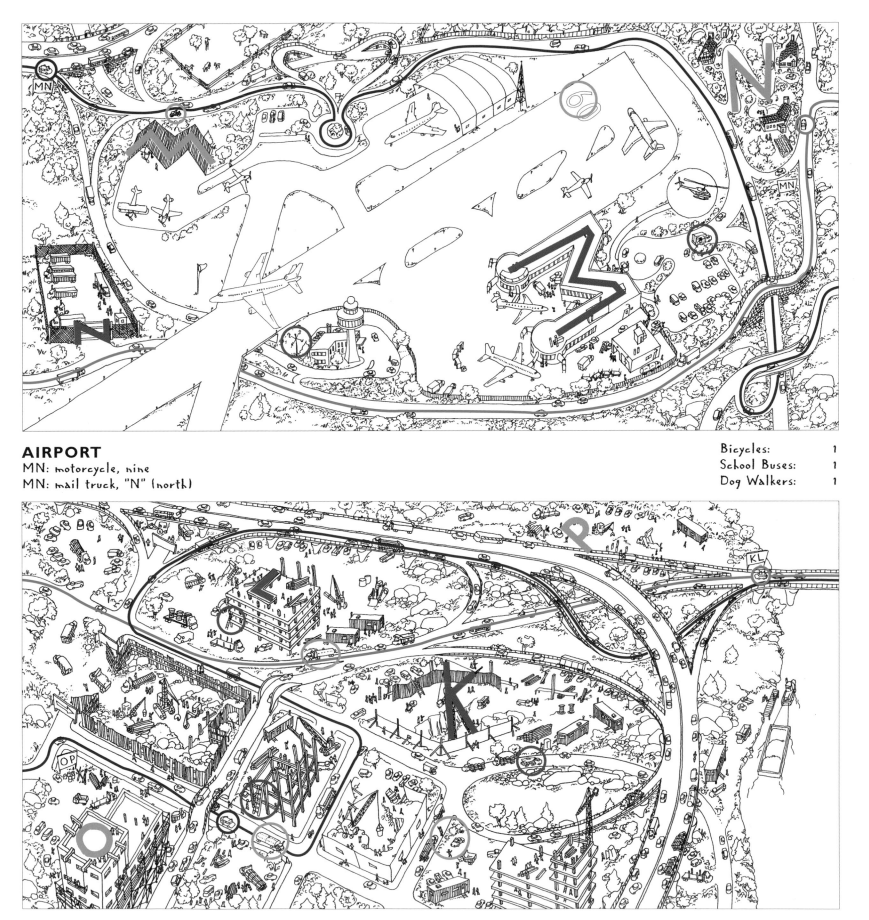

AIRPORT
MN: motorcycle, nine
MN: mail truck, "N" (north)

Bicycles: 1
School Buses: 1
Dog Walkers: 1

CONSTRUCTION
OP: oil trucks, police
KL: kayak, ladders

Bicycles: 1
School Buses: 1
Dog Walkers: 1

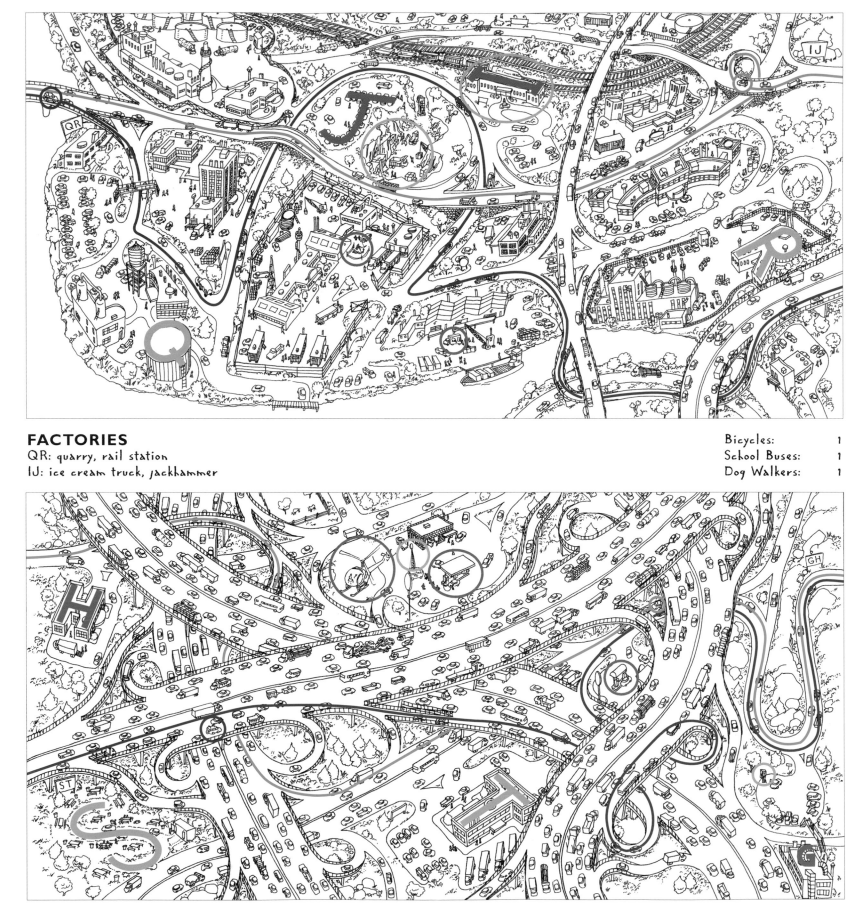

FACTORIES
QR: quarry, rail station
IJ: ice cream truck, jackhammer

Bicycles:	1
School Buses:	1
Dog Walkers:	1

FREEWAYS
ST: satellite dish, telephone booth
GH: gas stations, helicopter

Bicycles:	1
School Buses:	3
Dog Walkers:	1

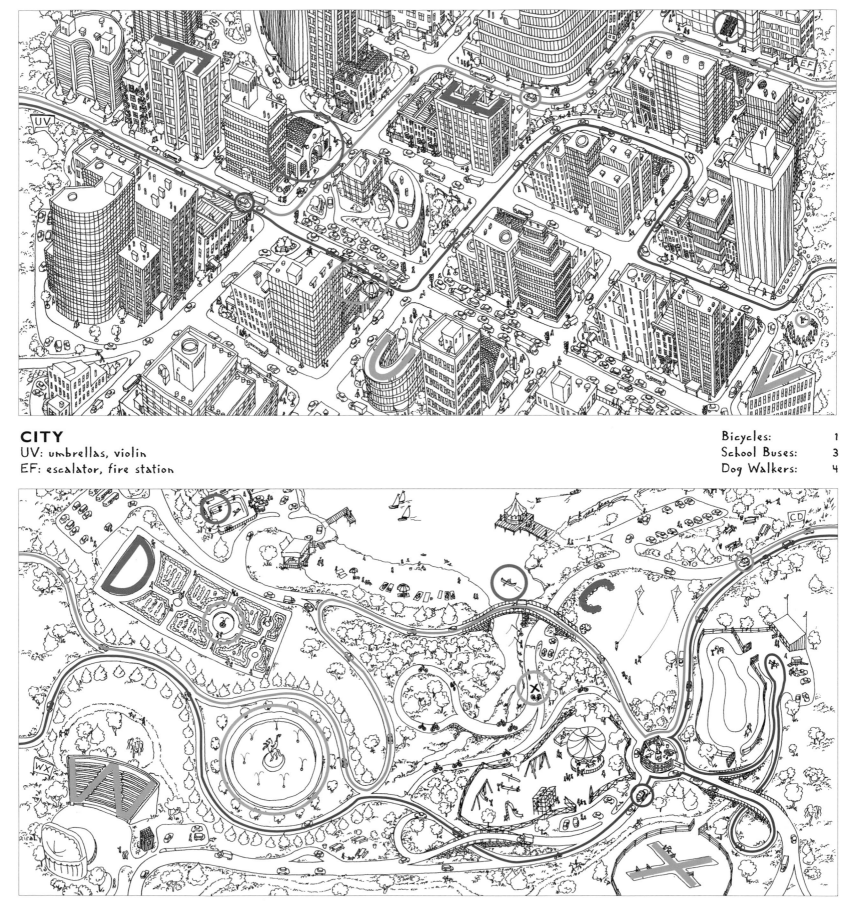

CITY
UV: umbrellas, violin
EF: escalator, fire station

Bicycles: 1
School Buses: 3
Dog Walkers: 4

PARK
WX: water fountains, "X" (bike crossing)
CD: canoe, diver

Bicycles: 11
School Buses: 3
Dog Walkers: 4

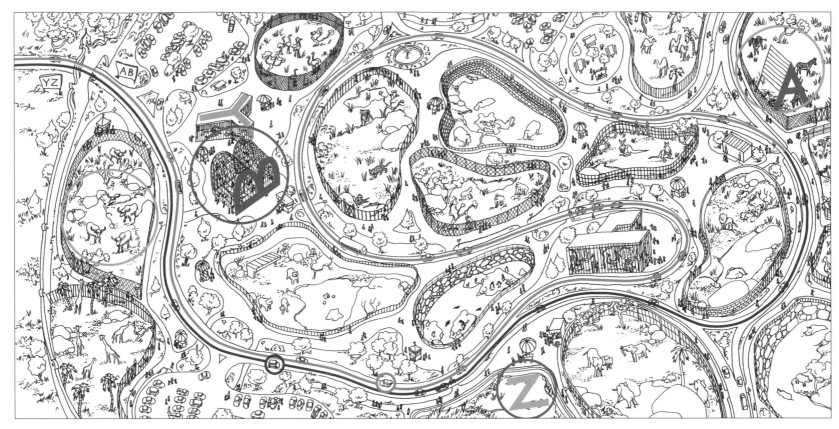

ZOO

YZ: yaks, zebras
AB: alligators, birds

Bicycles:	2
School Buses:	1
Dog Walkers:	1

See inside back cover for six punch-out vehicles to use on your journey...

OR MAKE YOUR OWN!

To Bo, who helps me
navigate the maze of life
—R. M.

Copyright © 2001 by Roxie Munro

SEASTAR BOOKS
A division of NORTH-SOUTH BOOKS INC.

First published in the United States by SeaStar Books, a division of North-South Books Inc., New York. Published simultaneously in Canada, Australia, and New Zealand by North-South Books, an imprint of Nord-Süd Verlag AG, Gossau Zürich, Switzerland.

Library of Congress Cataloging-in-Publication Data is available.
The artwork for this book was prepared by using watercolors and ink.

ISBN 1-58717-060-4 (reinforced trade binding)
1 2 3 4 5 6 7 8 9 10 RT

Printed in Singapore

For more information about our books, and the authors and artists who create them, visit our web site: www.northsouth.com